W9-ANT-376

"Dream Weaver"
Song written by Gary Wright
Courtesy of Universal Music Corp.
Used by Permission. All Rights Reserved.

LyricPop is a children's picture book collection by LyricVerse and Akashic Books.

lyricverse.

Published by Akashic Books
Song lyrics ©1975 Gary Wright
Illustrations ©2021 Rob Sayegh Jr.

ISBN: 978-1-61775-857-7
Library of Congress Control Number: 2020948257
First printing

Printed in China

Akashic Books
Brooklyn, New York
Twitter: @AkashicBooks
Facebook: AkashicBooks
E-mail: info@akashicbooks.com
Website: www.akashicbooks.com

dream weaver

SONG LYRICS BY **GARY WRIGHT**

ILLUSTRATIONS BY **ROB SAYEGH JR.**

I'VE JUST CLOSED MY EYES AGAIN
CLIMBED ABOARD THE DREAM WEAVER TRAIN

DRIVER TAKE AWAY MY WORRIES OF TODAY

AND LEAVE TOMORROW BEHIND

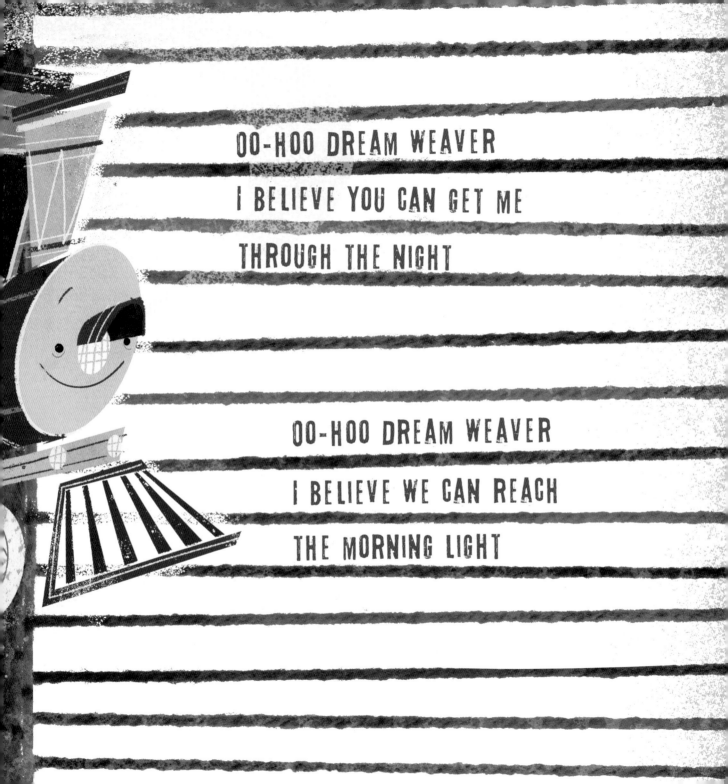

OO-HOO DREAM WEAVER

I BELIEVE YOU CAN GET ME

THROUGH THE NIGHT

OO-HOO DREAM WEAVER

I BELIEVE WE CAN REACH

THE MORNING LIGHT

FLY ME HIGH THROUGH THE STARRY SKIES

MAYBE TO AN ASTRAL PLANE

CROSS THE HIGHWAYS
OF FANTASY
HELP ME TO FORGET
TODAY'S PAIN

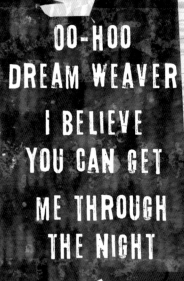

OO-HOO
DREAM WEAVER
I BELIEVE
YOU CAN GET

ME THROUGH
THE NIGHT

OO-HOO DREAM WEAVER
I BELIEVE WE CAN REACH
THE MORNING LIGHT

THOUGH THE DAWN MAY BE COMING SOON

THERE STILL MAY BE SOME TIME

FLY ME AWAY TO THE BRIGHT SIDE OF THE MOON

MEET ME ON THE OTHER SIDE

OO-HOO DREAM WEAVER
I BELIEVE YOU CAN GET
ME THROUGH THE NIGHT

OO-HOO DREAM WEAVER
I BELIEVE WE CAN REACH
THE MORNING LIGHT

DREAM WEAVER

DREAM WEAVER

ABOUT THE ARTISTS

Gary Wright is an American singer-songwriter, best known for his multiplatinum hits "Dream Weaver" and "Love Is Alive." Before his solo album *The Dream Weaver* was released in 1975, Wright played in the London music scene with the heavy rock band Spooky Tooth and also collaborated with both George Harrison and Ringo Starr. *The Dream Weaver* was certified platinum, with its hit single "Dream Weaver" reaching #2 on the *Billboard* Hot 100 chart. Wright continues to perform live as a solo act, as well as with both Spooky Tooth and Ringo Starr's All-Starr Band. His autobiography, *Dream Weaver: Music, Meditation, and My Friendship with George Harrison*, was published in 2014.

✺ ✺ ✺

Rob Sayegh Jr. is an author and illustrator who loves creating playful worlds with funny characters to make families giggle together. He is a professional snack taste-tester, falls in love with every dog he meets, and enjoys finding and creating new textures for his artwork. Sayegh has spent most of his life designing toys to encourage kids to constantly play, learn, and imagine new possibilities. He currently lives with his family in San Francisco, California. To see more of Sayegh's work, visit www.robsayart.com.

LOOK OUT FOR THESE LyricPop TITLES

The 59th Street Bridge Song (Feelin' Groovy)
SONG LYRICS BY PAUL SIMON • ILLUSTRATIONS BY KEITH HENRY BROWN

Paul Simon's groovy anthem to New York City provides a joyful basis for this live-for-the-day picture book.

African
SONG LYRICS BY PETER TOSH • ILLUSTRATIONS BY RACHEL MOSS

A beautiful children's picture book featuring the lyrics of Peter Tosh's global classic celebrating people of African descent.

(Sittin' on) The Dock of the Bay
SONG LYRICS BY OTIS REDDING AND STEVE CROPPER • IILLUSTRATIONS BY KAITLYN SHEA O'CONNOR

Otis Redding and Steve Cropper's timeless ode to never-ending days is given fresh new life in this heartwarming picture book.

Don't Stop
SONG LYRICS BY CHRISTINE McVIE • ILLUSTRATIONS BY NUSHA ASHJAEE

Christine McVie's classic song for Fleetwood Mac about keeping one's chin up and rolling with life's punches is beautifully adapted to an uplifting children's book.

Good Vibrations
SONG LYRICS BY MIKE LOVE AND BRIAN WILSON • ILLUSTRATIONS BY PAUL HOPPE

Mike Love and Brian Wilson's world-famous song for the Beach Boys, gloriously illustrated by Paul Hoppe, will bring smiles to the faces of children and parents alike.

Humble and Kind
SONG LYRICS BY LORI McKENNA • ILLUSTRATIONS BY KATHERINE BLACKMORE

Award-winning songwriter Lori McKenna's iconic song—as popularized by Tim McGraw—is the perfect basis for a picture book that celebrates family and togetherness.

I Will Survive
SONG LYRICS BY DINO FEKARIS AND FREDERICK J. PERREN • ILLUSTRATIONS BY KAITLYN SHEA O'CONNOR

Perren and Fekaris's disco hit sensation—popularized by Gloria Gaynor—comes to life as an empowering picture book featuring an alien princess living life on her own terms.